THE VERY PERSISTENT GAPPERS OF FRIP

THE
VERY
PERSISTENT
GAPPERS
of FRIP

George Saunders

illustrated by Lane Smith

Villard
New York

VILLARD BOOKS and colophon are registered trademarks
of Random House, Inc.

Library of Congress Cataloging-in-Publication Data
Saunders, George.
The very persistent gappers of Frip / George Saunders and Lane Smith.
p. cm.
ISBN 0-375-50383-8
I. Smith, Lane, ill. II. Title
PS3569.A7897 V47 2000
813.54—dc21   00-023131

Random House website address: www.villard.com

Printed on acid-free paper. Printed and bound
in Spain by Artes Graficas Toledo, S.A.U.

D.L. TO: 574-2000

24689753

First Edition

Special thanks to Natalie.

DESIGN BY MOLLY LEACH

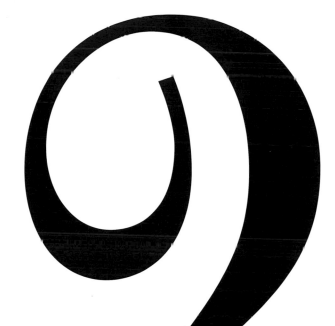

EVER HAD A BURR IN YOUR SOCK

A GAPPER'S LIKE THAT, ONLY BIGGER, about the size of a baseball, bright orange, with multiple eyes like the eyes on a potato. And gappers love goats. When a gapper gets near a goat it gives off a continual high-pitched happy shriek of pleasure that makes it impossible for the goat to sleep, and the goats get skinny and stop giving milk. And in towns that survive by selling goat milk, if there's no goat milk, there's no money, and if there's no money, there's no food or housing or clothing, and so, in gapper-infested towns, since nobody likes the idea of starving naked outdoors, it is necessary at all costs to keep the gappers off the goats.

SUCH A TOWN WAS FRIP.

Frip was three leaning shacks by the sea. Frip was three tiny goat-yards into which eight times a day the children of the shacks would trudge with gapper-brushes and cloth gapper-sacks that tied at the top. After brushing the gappers off the goats, the children would walk to a cliff at the edge of town and empty their gapper-sacks into the sea.

The gappers would sink to the bottom and immediately begin inching their way across the ocean floor, and three hours later would arrive again at Frip and split into three groups, one per goat-yard, only to be brushed off again by the same weary and discouraged children, who would stumble home and fall into their little beds for a few hours of sleep, dreaming, if they dreamed at all, of gappers putting *them* into sacks and dropping *them* into the sea.

In the shack closest to the sea lived a girl named Capable.

Earlier that year her mother had died. Since then, her father had very much liked things to stay as they were. At dusk Capable would find him in the yard, ordering the sun to stay up, then sitting sadly in the flower bed when the sun disobeyed him and went down anyway.

The last thing her mother had ever cooked
was rice, and now Capable's father insisted
that all his food be white. So in addition to
brushing gappers eight times a day and faith-
fully mending her gapper-sack, Capable also
had to mix sugar and milk and cliff-chalk
into a special white dye and spread it over
whatever she was cooking that night.

It was a hard life, and it made her tired.

"Father," she said one day, "maybe it's time
we moved. Away from the ocean. Away from
the gappers."

"My dear, I'm surprised at you," he said.
"This is our home. It has always been our
home. There have always been gappers, and
exhausted children brushing them off.

I myself was once an exhausted child brushing off gappers. It was lovely! The best years of my life. The way they fell to the sea from our bags! And anyway, what would you do with your time if there were no gappers?"

"Sleep," said Capable, whose eyes were deep dark pools.

"Ha ha, sleep, yes," said her father sadly, and went off for his afternoon nap.

Now gappers are not smart, but then again they are not all equally stupid. One day, at the bottom of the sea, one of the less-stupid gappers, who had a lump on one side of its

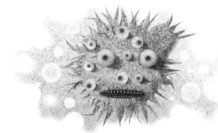

skull that was actually its somewhat larger-than-average brain sort of sticking out, calculated that, of the three houses in Frip, the reddish one—Capable's house—was about fifteen feet closer to the sea than the next-closest house, which, when you are the size of a baseball and have no legs and move around by crinkling and uncrinkling your extremely sensitive belly, is useful information.

So that night, instead of splitting into
three groups, the gappers moved in one very
large impressive shrieking group directly
into Capable's yard.

There were approximately fifteen hundred gappers living in the sea near Frip. Each Frip family had about ten goats. Therefore, there would normally be about five hundred gappers per yard, or fifty gappers per goat. Tonight, however, with all fifteen hundred gappers in Capable's yard, there were approximately one hundred fifty gappers per goat. Since the average goat can carry about sixty gappers before it drops to its knees and keels over on one side with a mortified look on its face, when Capable came out to brush gappers that night, she found every single one of her goats lying on its side with a mortified look on its face, completely covered with shrieking orange gappers.

When the other Frip children came out to brush gappers, they found they had no gappers.

So they went back inside and fell asleep.

IN THE HOUSE NEXT DOOR LIVED
Mrs. Bea Romo, a singer, whose children,
two sons, were also singers. They all sang in a
proud and angry way, as if yelling at someone, their faces bright red.

"It's a miracle!" Mrs. Romo shouted next
morning, when she came out and discovered
that her yard was free of gappers. "This is
wonderful! Capable, dear, you poor thing.
The miracle didn't happen to you, did it? I
feel so sorry for you. God has been good to
us, by taking our gappers away. Why? I can't
say. God knows what God is doing, I guess! I
suppose we must somehow deserve it! Boys!
Boys! Come out and look!"

And her boys, Robert and Gilbert, came out and looked.

"What?" said Robert, who was himself only slightly brighter than a gapper.

"I don't get it," said Gilbert, who was exactly as bright as a gapper.

"No gappers, boys!" said Bea. "See? No more gapper-brushing!"

"So what are you saying, Ma?" said Robert. "Are you saying we don't have to brush gappers as long as there aren't any?"

"Is that what you're saying, Ma?" said Gilbert.

"Boys, it's a good thing you're such excellent singers," said Bea Romo, sort of rolling her eyes at Capable. "Because you're certainly not going to win any brain awards."

"Well, I don't want a brain award," said Robert.

"Me too," said Gilbert. "I don't want a brain award either."

"Unless they give money with it," said Robert.

"Do they give money with it?" said Gilbert. "In that case maybe I'll take it."

"Money or candy," said Gilbert. "Or a trophy."

"Or a medal," said Robert.

"Unless they pin the medal right directly into your brain," said Gilbert. "In that case, no, I don't want it."

"Me too," said Robert. "If they're going to stick a pin into my brain about it, forget it."

"Boys, stop talking," said Bea Romo. "Stop talking now, go inside and sing."

"Okay," said Robert. "But no brain awards."

"And that's final," said Gilbert.

And the Romo boys went back inside and
sang some more angry scales, after which

they argued about which of them sang the
best, after which they wrestled about which

of them sang the best and there was the
sound of some wooden thing breaking,
possibly a piano bench.

* * *

LATER THAT DAY CAPABLE CAME
out to brush gappers and found Mrs. Romo
saying heave-ho to a team of several strong
men from Fritch, the next town over, who
had their shoulders to the Romos' little
green shack. It was tilted way up and
Capable could see dark dirt and worms
underneath and a pair of old shoes.

"Hello dear!" Mrs. Romo said. "Hope you
don't mind—I'm moving my house as far
away from yours as I possibly can! After we
spoke earlier, it occurred to me that the only
thing separating my yard from your yard is a
picket fence. Which gappers could easily
squeeze through! And one thing I don't need
at this point is a yard full of gappers! I suppose they don't bother you anymore, you're
probably used to them, you probably even
take a kind of crude enjoyment in them, but
my boys are made of more sensitive stuff,
and mustn't be distracted from their singing
careers! To the lot-line, fellows! Lift, men,
you can do it!"

And the men succeeded in lifting the
house and moving it very very close to the
third and final house in Frip, which belonged
to Sid and Carol Ronsen, who stood in their
yard with looks of dismay on their nearly
identical frowning faces.

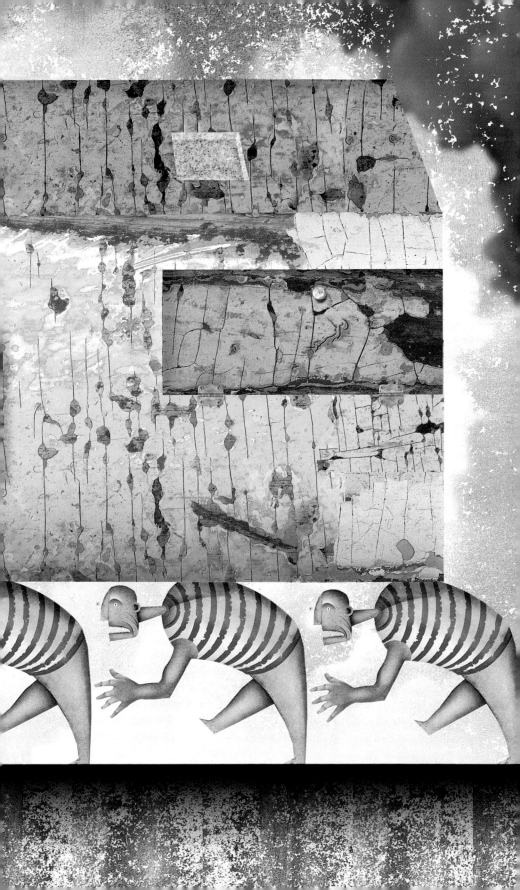

"See here!" said Sid Ronsen.

"See here!" said Carol Ronsen. "What are you doing, Bea?"

"What in the world are you doing, Bea?" said Sid. "Good Lord! Moving your house so close? You're crowding our little house. Do you see it? Our little house is this blue one here, the one your house is now nearly touching, Bea."

And it was true. The houses were now very very close. A person could easily hop from roof to roof. The Romo boys were doing just this. They were hopping from roof to roof, singing in angry voices, while the Ronsen girls, Beverly and Gloria, craned their heads out the window with their fingers in their ears.

"I'm still on my property," said Mrs. Romo.

"Good Lord," said Sid.

"Good Lord, Bea," said Carol. "You could look right in on us. You could look right in on us being naked in our own private bathroom."

"Don't worry, I won't!" said Mrs. Romo. "Although you will probably hear us singing from time to time!"

"Lucky us," said Sid Ronsen.

And immediately, Sid Ronsen hired the same five men to move *his* house to the far edge of *his* property.

Now the distance between his house and the Romo house was exactly the same as it had been that morning.

It was as if the world had tipped, and the Romo and Ronsen houses had slid over, but Capable's house had stayed where it was.

✳ ✳ ✳

OVER THE NEXT FEW WEEKS
Capable tried everything she could think of
to get rid of the gappers

She tried hiding the goats under blankets,

setting the goats on tables,

building fences around the goats,

shaving the goats, but nothing worked.

She moved the goats inside, but the gappers only squeezed under the door and blundered into the dye vat and left white streaks across the floor as they chased the worried-looking goats around the kitchen.

Finally her goats stopped giving milk altogether, which meant no milk and no cheese, and no money from selling the milk and cheese, which meant that Capable and her father were reduced to eating dandelions, which she first had to paint white.

"Father," she said late one night. "I can't keep up. Our goats are dying. We're going to have to ask the neighbors for help."

"Have we ever done that before?" he said.

"We've never needed help before," said Capable.

"Well I'm against it," he said. "If we haven't done it before, it stands to reason that this is the first time we've done it, which means that, relative to what we've done in the past, this is different, which I am very much against, as I always have been, as you well know. I have consistently been very very consistent about this."

Then he went back to sleep and Capable went out to the yard. Twenty times she filled her sack with gappers and walked to the cliff. As she brushed and bagged she thought of her mother, and while thinking of her mother she seemed to hear her mother's voice, saying: Honey, if you need help, ask for help, you're not alone in this world, you sweet little goof.

So she went inside and wrote a note to the Romos and the Ronsens:

Dear friends, it said, *we need your help. The gappers are too much for me. They're killing our goats. Please help, I beg you, your friend Capable.*

Then she left a copy for the Romos and a copy for the Ronsens, and went to sleep happy, feeling that tomorrow things would get better.

✹ ✹ ✹

"GOOD LORD!" SAID SID RONSEN next morning, standing by his fence, reading the note. "What is the meaning of this? What is she thinking? Are those gappers our gappers? Are those goats our goats?"

"Good Lord!" said Carol Ronsen. "They certainly are not. They are her goats and her gappers, as indicated by the fact that they are in her yard. Is her yard our yard? I think not."

"I feel that our yards are our yards," said Bea Romo.

"Quite right!" said Sid Ronsen. "Well said, Bea."

"I for one," said Carol Ronsen, and then forgot what she was going to say, and poked Sid Ronsen, who almost always knew what she had been about to say.

"I for one," he said, poking her back, out of habit, "do not intend to stand idly by while my poor daughters, Beverly and Gloria, who only recently were freed from gapper-duty, go marching out of my yard, into her yard, and lend a hand. What sort of father would I be? What kind of message would I be sending? Wouldn't I be saying: Girls, I don't value you, I think you should work like dogs to solve a problem that isn't even yours? Preposterous! I refuse to say that! I am very sorry that Capable's luck has gone bad, but, come to think of it, I for one do not believe in luck. Do you know what I do believe?"

"You don't believe in luck," said Carol Ronsen, who was quite thrilled that what she had been going to say had turned out to be so very long and opinionated.

"I believe we make our own luck in this world," said Sid Ronsen. "I believe that, when my yard suddenly is free of gappers, why, that is because of something good I have done. Because, as both of you ladies know, I have always been a hard worker."

"As have I," said Bea Romo. "I too have always been a hard worker, as have my boys, and look: No gappers, just like you. I suppose one might say that we too have made our own luck. With our hard work."

"Work, work, work," said Carol Ronsen.

"Perhaps I should compose a response," said Sid Ronsen.

"That would be super," said Bea Romo.

So Sid Ronsen composed the following response:

Dear Capable, it said, *we are in receipt of your let-ter of the other day, that other day, whenever that day was, when you sent that letter that you sent us. We regret to inform you that, although we are very sympa-thetic to your significant hardships, don't you think it would be better if you took responsibility for your own life? We feel strongly that, once you rid your goats of gappers, as we have, you will feel better about yourself, and also, we will feel better about you. Not that we're saying we're better than you, necessarily, it's just that, since gappers are bad, and since you and you alone now have them, it only stands to reason that you are not, perhaps, quite as good as us. Not that we hate you! We don't. We sort of even like you. Just please get rid of those gappers! Prove that you can do it, just as we proved we could do it, and at that time, and that time only, please come over, and won't that be fun, all of us standing around the fire, sharing a laugh about those bad old days when we all had gappers.*

Love, Your Neighbors.

Sid crept to Capable's mailbox and slipped the note in.

* * *

THAT AFTERNOON, MRS. ROMO
finished her usual afternoon session of
shouting at her boys for not doing their
afternoon scales, then stepped out onto what
she called her veranda, which was a little
square of hard-packed dirt where the cat
liked to leave its chewed-up spitty toys.

Walking by was Capable, looking mad,
leading her goats on a rope.

With Capable was her father, muttering
and shaking his head.

"Hello, dear," said Mrs. Romo. "How quaint that you've tied all your goats together. They look so cute. Why did you do it? Just being silly? Taking them on a little tour of the town?"

"No," said Capable. "I'm giving up."

"Why say it so grumpy?" said Bea Romo. "And what do you mean you're giving up?"

"I'm taking them to Fritch, to sell," Capable said. "It's too hard here, and nobody's helping us."

"Do you mean me?" said Bea Romo.

"I hope you don't mean us," said Sid Ronsen, leaning out the window with shaving cream on his face.

"Did you not get our letter?" said Bea Romo.

"Did you not get my letter?" said Sid Ronsen.

"I have to say it's a strange idea," said Carol Ronsen. "I have to say it makes me somewhat angry. That you should expect us to do your work. I mean, do you cover my roses? Do you polish my antiques?"

"Do you force my boys to sing their scales?" said Bea Romo.

"Do you trim my nose hairs?" said Sid Ronsen.

"And what will you do then?" said Carol Ronsen. "Having sold your goats?"

"Fish," said Capable.

"Good Lord!" said Sid Ronsen.

This was a shocker. The people of Frip did not fish. They had stopped fishing long ago, when Sid Ronsen's great-grandfather had acquired the town's first goat. Sid's great-grandfather had been the richest man in town, and once he got a goat, everyone wanted a goat, and fishing went out of style, and now fishing was considered something one did only if one was not bright enough to acquire a goat.

"Fish for what?" said Bea Romo. "For fish? With a hook? A hook and some bait? Some bait on a hook, which you throw into the sea?"

"To think it's come to this," said Capable's father. "To think that my daughter is going to start fishing, which is something she's never done before."

"You must be heartbroken," said Sid
Ronsen.

"I've been crying about it all night," said
Capable's father. "Which is why my mus-
tache is so wet and my nose is so red, which I
have to say is completely unprecedented."

"I've done my best," said Capable. "But
look at these goats."

Everyone looked at the goats, which were
skinny and jittery and kept glancing ner-
vously out at the ocean.

"If you want my advice?" said Sid Ronsen. "Work harder. Actually, no, don't work harder, work smarter. Be more efficient than you've ever been before. In fact, be more efficient than is physically possible. I know that's what I'd do."

"That's also what I would do," said Bea Romo.

"Me too," said Carol Ronsen.

"I certainly wouldn't start fishing about it," said Sid Ronsen.

But Capable knew she had tried her best, and her best hadn't worked, and remembered her mother once saying: Just because a lot of people are saying the same thing loudly over and over, doesn't mean it's true.

So she kissed her father on the cheek and walked her goats out of Frip, and a few hours later returned with a fishing pole and some hooks and a big heavy book called *How to Fish for Fish*.

* * *

R EMEMBER THAT LESS-STUPID
gapper with the brain poking out the side of
his head?

That night he deduced that the reddish
Frip shack, the one they had come to love so
well, was now totally without goats. He
deduced this by systematically leading his
team of fifteen hundred gappers blindly
around Capable's yard for approximately six
hours. Once he had confirmed the total
absence of goats, he led his team into the
Romos' yard, where he found ten fat com-
placent goats, who were soon lying on their
sides, mortified, covered with bright orange
gappers making the usual high-pitched joyful shrieking noise, which woke Bea Romo
from a sweet dream in which she was
engaged to a handsome man who loved to
hear her sing. She was singing and singing,
when suddenly her fiancé turned into a vacuum cleaner and, apparently in response to
her excellent singing, began making a high-
pitched joyful shrieking noise. The shrieking

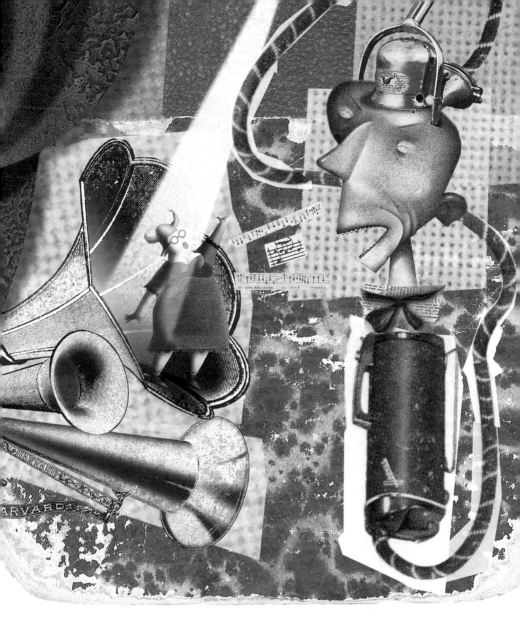

was louder than her singing, however, so
Bea Romo stepped on the little switch on
her fiancé's foot, to make him stop shrieking,
so he could better hear her singing. When
this didn't work, she woke with an angry
look on her face, having decided never to
date a vacuum cleaner again, especially one

who didn't properly appreciate her singing. She then realized with some alarm that, even though she had stepped very firmly on her fiancé's foot, the high-pitched joyful shrieking noise still hadn't stopped.

Imagine her surprise when she went to the window and saw her goats lying on their sides, mortified, covered with gappers.

Bea Romo let out a high-pitched shrieking noise of her own that was not a bit joyful.

"Good Lord!" said Sid Ronsen from his bed. "Is that Bea? Is that Bea shrieking? Is she shrieking or singing?"

"It's always so hard to tell," said Carol Ronsen.

They rushed to the window and saw the Romo boys, Robert and Gilbert, frantically brushing gappers, just like in the old days.

"Robert! Gilbert!" said Sid Ronsen. "See here! Boys, how did this happen?"

But Robert and Gilbert were too breathless and sweaty to answer.

"Oh, Sid," said Carol Ronsen. "Check our goats. Are our goats fine?"

"I am happy to say that our goats appear to be fine," Sid said. "They are actually standing at the fence, watching Robert and Gilbert. Sort of smiling. Can goats smile? Our goats appear to be smiling."

"But no gappers?" said Carol Ronsen.

"No gappers," said Sid Ronsen.

"Thank God," said Carol Ronsen. "We are so blessed."

"I feel like praying," said Sid Ronsen. "I feel like thanking God for giving us whatever trait we have that keeps us so free of gappers."

"We should," said Carol Ronsen. "We should pray."

And the Ronsens prayed, thanking God for making them the sort of people they were, the sort of people who had no gappers, and they prayed that God would forgive Bea for not being that sort of person, and would have mercy on her, and, in His infinite mercy, would make Bea into a better sort of person, and take all her gappers away.

* * *

MEANWHILE CAPABLE WAS
teaching herself to fish. All day she stood on
the beach in a pair of dumpy green overalls.
Sometimes she practiced getting her line
caught in a tree, sometimes she practiced
peeling her worm off her forehead while
feeling grateful that she hadn't just succeeded in hooking her own eyebrow, other
times she practiced sitting frustrated and
near tears in the sand.

   At one point, having just knocked herself
down by trying to reel in her own shoe,
which unfortunately at that time was still on
her foot, she looked up to see Beverly and
Gloria Ronsen staring down at her with
their eyebrows held very high.

"You should be glad we're not boys," said
Beverly.

"Boys would not like that, what you just
did," said Gloria. "Boys do not like girls who
wear overalls and knock themselves over
with their own fishing thingamabobs."

"Boys like girls who wear nice dresses and
who, if they absolutely have to fall over, do so
only after being pushed over by a boy who's
just kidding, who only knocked them over to
show how much he liked them," said Beverly.
"At least that's been my experience."

"Yes," said Gloria. "Although some boys
might not mind a girl who falls over, if that girl
giggled a bit and needed his help to get up."

"True," said Beverly. "Although the type of boy I like? He is the type of boy who likes the type of girl who not only never falls over, but rarely even moves. Because she is so graceful. She just stands there absolutely still while looking very pretty. Such as this."

"Such as this here," said Gloria. "What we're going to do right now."

And both Ronsen girls stood very still, and looked sort of pretty, if you like the kind of

girl who, to look sort of pretty, has to stand
very still

"Why do you care so much what boys like?"
said Capable, and at this point Beverly and
Gloria stopped standing perfectly still in order
to gasp, turn red in the face, then fold and
unfold their largish ears several times with
their fingers as if there were some blockage
that had kept them from hearing her correctly.

"I totally care what boys like!" said Beverly.
"Especially cute boys."

"I even care what ugly boys like," said
Gloria.

"Because who knows," said Beverly. "An
ugly boy might turn out to be cute later."

"Or he might have a cute friend," said
Gloria.

"Take Bob Bern," said Gloria. "He's ugly.
His nose is about a foot long. But guess who
he's friends with?"

"Bernie Bin!" said Beverly. "Oh my God! Is
Bernie's nose ever not a foot long! His nose
is so cute! It's just the right length."

At that moment Capable caught her first
fish, which came skittering across the beach
like a silver coin that had suddenly come to life
and was trying to get a hook out of its mouth.

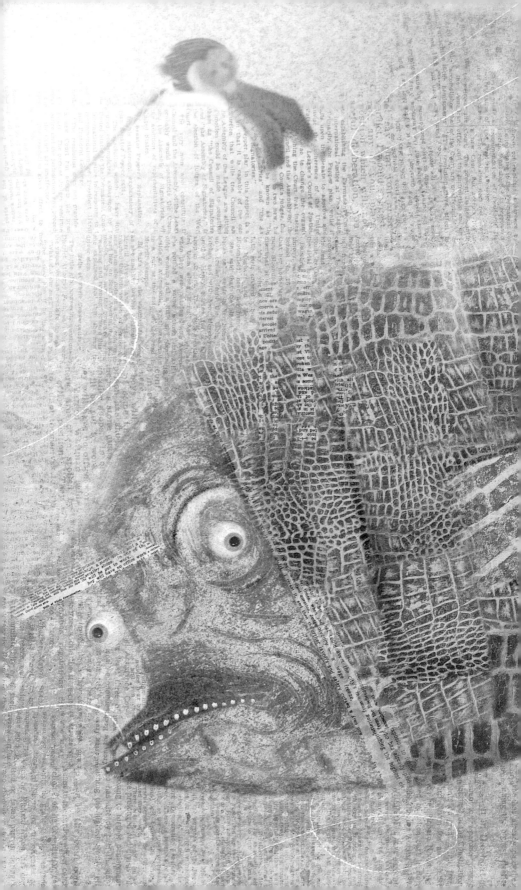

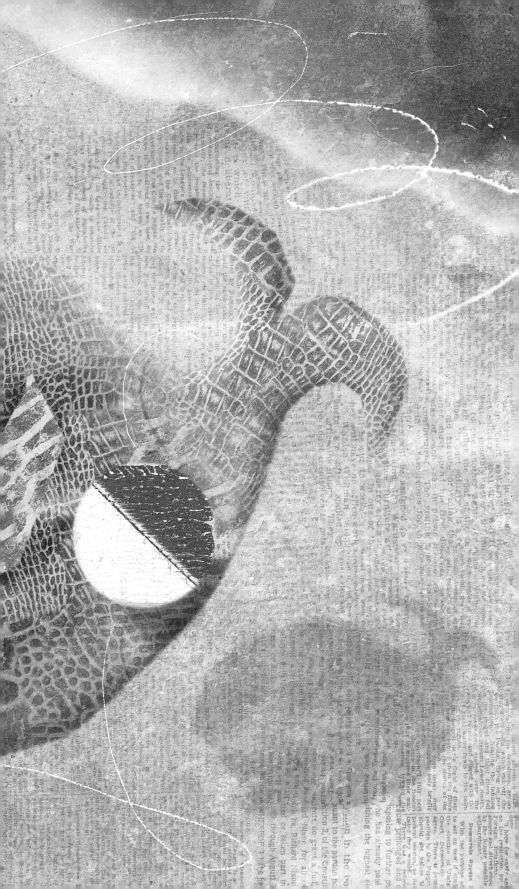

"Gosh, yuck!" said Gloria. "Watch it! That thing on that hook nearly brushed right against my new tights!"

"One thing we do not need is fish-goo on our new tights," said Beverly, and led Gloria off the beach.

The fishing was good.

By ten Capable had caught enough fish for a nice dinner. The rest of the morning she swam and slept. In the early afternoon, she swam some more, made a sandcastle, and day-dreamed a bit. She daydreamed about the old days when her father used to make her mother laugh by holding radishes in his eye sockets. She daydreamed about dressing up the Romo boys in goat suits and locking them in a closet full of gappers. In the late afternoon she day-dreamed further, slept again, woke up, went for a swim, made a second sandcastle, then walked home happy, dragging behind her a huge gapper-sack full of fish.

* * *

BY NOON THE NEXT DAY, BEA
Romo's goats had stopped giving milk.

"Uh, Carol?" she said that afternoon at the
fence. "Why not send over your girls? We'll
make a party of it. A cookie-and-milk party.
And Carol? Do you have any cookies? And
do you have any milk? For the party? Oh
Carol, I'm so worried. My boys are so tired,
they never sing anymore, they only fall asleep
in the yard, with those horrible gappers
crawling all over their arms, the arms with
which they used to gesture so beautifully
while they sang. I worry about their singing
careers. Even I myself am singing less, I'm so
worried about them."

"Not everyone can be a singer, Bea," said
Carol. "We all must accept our lot in life.
Some of us are singers and some of us are
gapper-brushers, and it seems to me that,
if you would simply happily accept the fact
that your kids are gapper-brushers, and
always will be, gosh, just think how happy
you'd be."

"Oh Carol," said Bea, starting to weep.
"Things are going badly for us."

"Life is mysterious," said Carol.

"Isn't it though," said Bea, and tried to get
a hug from Carol. But Carol, afraid that a
gapper or two might be hiding under Bea's

tremendous operatic gown, pretended to
suddenly sneeze, taking two very large steps
back from the fence.

"But you'll come to the party?" said Bea.
"The milk-and-cookie party? And you'll
bring milk and cookies, and your kids, who'll
bring their gapper-brushes? Oh gosh, won't
it be fun?"

"Well Bea," said Carol. "To tell the truth,
that doesn't sound like all that much fun,
really. Us brushing your gappers? When we
ourselves have none? And with gappers
being so disgusting and all? What fun is that?
Do you see what I mean?"

"Well, aren't you suddenly a snoot," said Bea Romo.

"A snoot?" cried Carol. "Are you calling me a snoot? Good Lord!"

"Who's calling who a snoot?" said Sid Ronsen, emerging from a bush he'd been trimming.

"Bea called me a snoot!" said Carol Ronsen.

"I think I'm going to cry," said Bea Romo.

"Oh brother," said Sid Ronsen. "First you call my wife a snoot, and then you start crying? Good Lord. You'd think Carol would be the crying one. Carol, come inside at once. I won't have my wife being called a snoot by someone with so many gappers. The nerve!"

And the Ronsens went inside.

Bea Romo stayed outside, thinking about possibly starting to cry. But since no one was around except the fifteen hundred gappers who just that minute were squeezing through her fence, she decided not to cry, but instead went inside and called the team of very strong men from Fritch, and asked could they come to her house first thing next morning.

FIRST THING NEXT MORNING
Carol and Sid Ronsen looked out their bed-
room window to find the team of very strong
men from Fritch walking past their house
very slowly, with shaky knees and red faces,
and sweat flying off their trembling arms,
and Bea Romo's house on their shoulders.

Just past the Ronsens' house, the strong
men set the Romo house down, brushed
off their hands, wiped their foreheads,
and accepted a big wad of money from
Bea Romo.

"See here!" said Sid Ronsen. "What are you
doing, Bea? Good Lord! Why are you putting
your house on the other side of our house, in
that vacant lot, the vacant lot by the swamp?"

"None of your beeswax, you snoot," said Bea Romo.

"Again with the snoot talk," said Carol Ronsen.

"Fine, Bea!" said Sid Ronsen. "If you want to live in a vacant lot, live in a vacant lot. It's no skin off our noses. Only stop calling us snoots!"

"And don't start in again with that awful singing," said Carol Ronsen.

A few hours later, that less-stupid gapper with the sticking-out brain led his gappers into the former Romo yard, found it goatless, and proceeded directly into the Ronsen yard.

Sid Ronsen was making lunch when he heard the high-pitched joyful shrieking and literally dropped his omelet on the dog, who quickly ate it.

"Good Lord!" Sid Ronsen shouted. "Girls! Get out there and start brushing. Brush like the wind, girls! This is terrible! Just awful. I blame Bea!"

"Don't blame me!" shouted Bea, standing at her window in her big operatic gown. "Accept your lot in life! Ha ha! You snoots. Let's see how you like it. Just look at my goats now."

"Good Lord!" said Carol Ronsen. "Bea's goats appear to be smiling."

"How about our goats?" said Sid Ronsen. "Do they appear to be smiling?"

"I can't tell," said Carol Ronsen. "There are too many gappers on their faces for me to see their mouths."

"Good Lord!" said Sid Ronsen. "We'll see about this, Bea! Two can play this game!"

And he rushed out of his house in his bathrobe and gave a big wad of money to the team of very strong men from Fritch, who, though still out of breath, carried his house past the Romo house, to the lip of the swamp.

After which Bea Romo paid the team of very strong men from Fritch to carry her house past the Ronsen house, literally into the swamp.

After which Sid Ronsen paid the team of very strong men from Fritch to carry his house past the Romo house, even further into the swamp.

This went on well into the afternoon, at which time the Romo and Ronsen houses were so far into the swamp that the Romos and the Ronsens could only stay dry by sitting on the peaks of their respective roofs, surrounded by their children and their goats and a few treasured household items.

Plus they were all completely out of money.

"Good-bye, folks!" said the leader of the team of very strong men from Fritch. "Have a nice day! And thanks for all the money!"

By now it was getting dark
and cold, so Sid Ronsen led his wife and children and goats off the roof, and they swam,
shivering, with looks of disgust on their faces,
through the swamp, followed by the scowling
shivering disgusted Romos and the scowling
shivering disgusted Romo goats.

At that moment Capable came up from
the sea with her big gapper-sack full of fish.

"What are those you have there?" said Carol Ronsen. "Are those fish? Fish you caught in the actual sea?"

"They don't look half-bad," said Bea Romo. "Actually they look sort of yummy. You know what might be fun? Maybe you could teach me and Robert and Gilbert to fish. Maybe, for fun, you could, you know, lend us a pole, and some worms, and sort of teach us to fish."

"And maybe you could also teach us to fish," said Sid Ronsen.

"And maybe also we could all live with you awhile?" said Carol Ronsen. "Just until we can sell our goats in Fritch and use the money to get our houses out of the swamp?"

"Ha ha!" said Sid Ronsen. "Somehow our houses ended up in that darn swamp!"

Capable looked at her neighbors, who were shivering and covered with swamp muck, and remembered the way they had all refused to help her.

Then she went into her house and shut the door.

She made a fire and cooked the fish. She sat down with the plate of fish in front of her window. She watched the Romos and Ronsens swim back across the swamp and remount their houses. She watched Robert Romo's shoe slip off and fall in the muck. She watched Sid Ronsen sitting with his head in his hands, possibly weeping, and Carol Ronsen sort of consoling him, by patting him on the back.

And she soon found that it was not all that much fun being the sort of person who eats a big dinner in a warm house while others shiver on their roofs in the dark.

That is, it was fun at first, but then got gradually less fun, until it was really no fun at all.

"Father," she said. "I guess we'll be having some company."

"What in the world?" he said. "Our house is so small, and there are so many of them. We have so little, and they'll use so much. This is a really big change. It makes a lot of extra work."

"Yes it is," said Capable. "Yes it does."

"But we're still doing it?" he said.

"Yes we are," she said, and called the neighbors in, and put water on for tea, because she knew that tea would taste good to people who'd recently been swimming in a freezing mucky swamp.

Then she cooked up a bunch more fish, remembering to paint a few white for her father.

Who at that moment said something amazing:

"You remind me of your mother," he said. "So generous and all."

Then he did something amazing:

He ate an unpainted fish.

SO THE NEXT MORNING, AND EVERY morning after that, Capable and her father and the Romos and the Ronsens went down to the sea and fished.

AND LIFE GOT BETTER.

Not perfect, but better. The Ronsen girls still sometimes stood completely motionless in order to look somewhat pretty; the Romo boys still argued, often about who was a better worm-finder, after which they wrestled

about who was a better worm-finder, after which they argued about who'd gotten more sand down his underwear during the wrestling, after which they hopped up and down, comparing the amount of sand that came dribbling out of their underwear; Mrs. Romo still burst into song from time to time, prompting the Ronsens to cover their ears, after which Mrs. Romo would sing louder, sort of pursuing the wincing Ronsens down the beach; but generally, on most days, everyone was happier.

Except of course the fish.

AND THE GAPPERS.

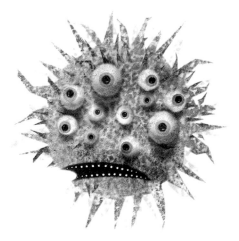

For weeks afterward, the gappers came sadly into town, looking for the goats.

But the goats were in Fritch, fat and happy.

Finally that less-stupid gapper, the one with the sticking-out brain, called a meeting. Seeing as how there were no longer any goats in Frip, he proposed that they stop loving goats. The goats had never returned their affections. The goats had taken them for granted. Goats stunk, actually. What was the point of loving someone who only nipped at you with its sharp yellow teeth whenever you joyously shrieked because you were happy to see it? It was an outrage. They'd been played for fools. Would it not, he proposed, be more prudent for them to love something that might actually love them back, some-thing solid and reliable, something that was actually still present in Frip?

What did he have in mind? the other gappers asked. What was still in Frip that might
possibly love them back?

Fences, the brighter gapper replied. And
he began singing the praises of the attractive
yet reliable fences of Frip, which never, to his
knowledge, had nipped anything with their
teeth, not having teeth, and which never, to
his knowledge, had even nipped anything
with their gates, but had only stood with
great dignity in all sorts of weather, looking
out very calmly to sea, as if waiting for something wonderful to emerge from the sea and
begin madly loving them.

So the gappers took a vote. And though
they were not in perfect agreement—one
believed they should begin loving wadded-
up pieces of paper, another believed they
should begin loving turtles, particularly turtles who were dying, particularly dying turtles who nevertheless kept a positive
attitude—the gappers still very much
admired and trusted that less-stupid gapper,
and voted to begin madly loving fences.

Which is how Frip came to be what it
is today: a seaside town known for its
relatively happy fisherpeople and its bright
orange shrieking fences.

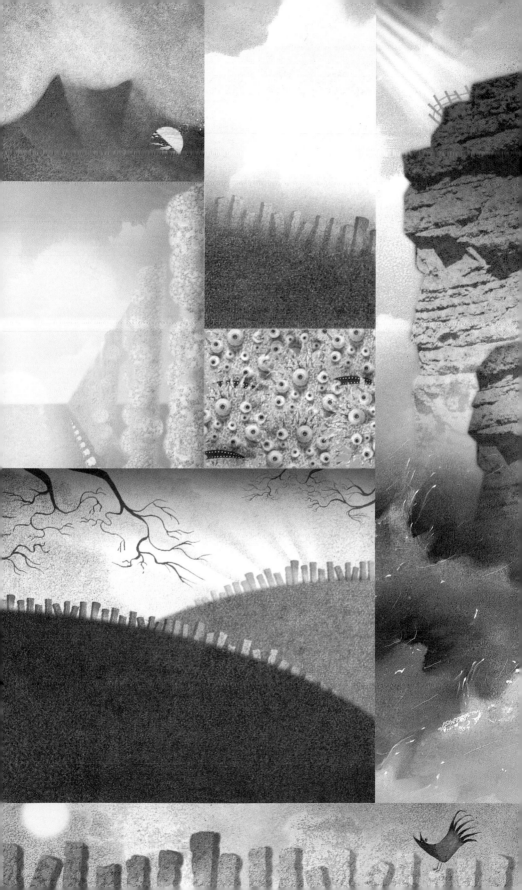

THE END.

ABOUT THE AUTHOR

GEORGE SAUNDERS is the author of two short-story collections, *Pastoralia* and *CivilWarLand in Bad Decline*, a finalist for the 1996 PEN/Hemingway Award. His work has received two National Magazine Awards and three times been included in O. Henry Awards collections. He teaches in the creative writing program at Syracuse University.

ABOUT THE ILLUSTRATOR

LANE SMITH has illustrated several number-one national bestsellers, including *The True Story of the 3 Little Pigs!*, *The Stinky Cheese Man*, Dr. Seuss's *Hooray for Diffendoofer Day*, and *James and the Giant Peach*. Smith has twice won *The New York Times*'s Best Illustrated Book of the Year award and in 1993 he received a Caldecott Honor. He is married to Molly Leach, the designer of this and many other books.